OPAL DUNN is widely known as a specialist in early first and second language development. She works as a consultant to the Council of Europe on children's bilingual education and acted as Chief Consultant to Linguaphone's prize-winning new story-based course, *Children's English*. Her previous books for Frances Lincoln are *Un Deux Trois – First French Rhymes*, *Hippety-Hop, Hippety-Hay – Growing with Rhymes from Birth to Age 3*, *Acker Backa Boo! Games to Say and Play from Around the World* and *Number Rhymes to Say and Play*.
Opal lives in north London.

CATHY GALE has written and illustrated more than 20 books for children, including *What Goes Snap?*, *Football Fun* and *A Brave Knight to the Rescue* (all Walker), and the Tiny Teethers series (Campbell Books).
This is her first book for Frances Lincoln.
Cathy lives in London, WC1.

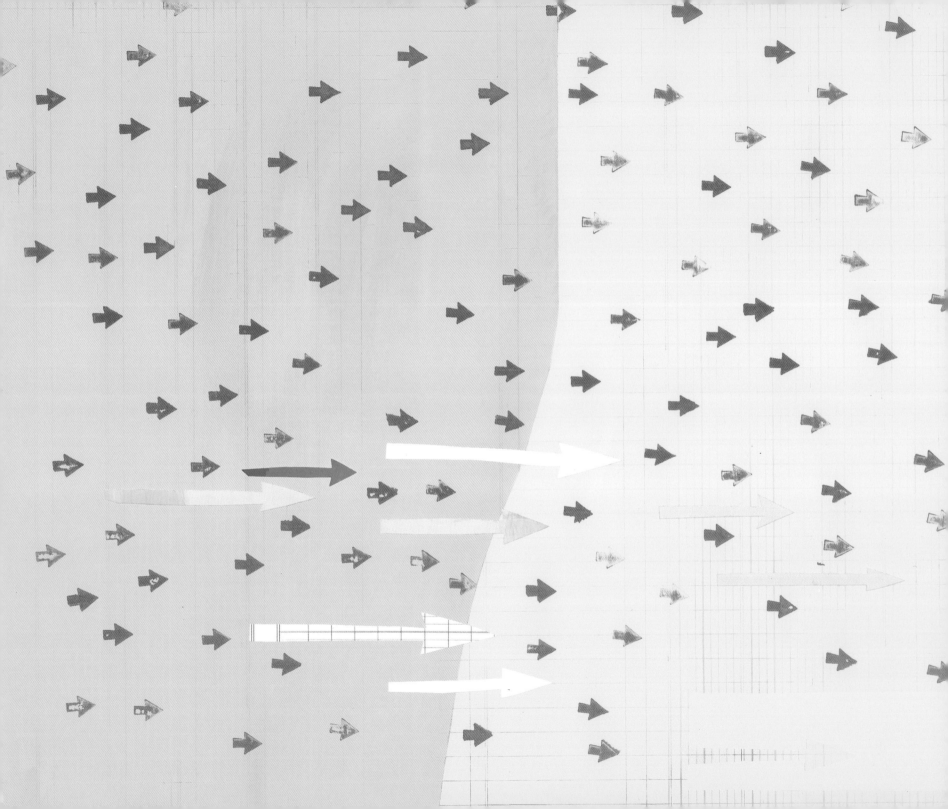

Dear Parents, Grandparents, Carers and Teachers,

Young children are born language learners. They pick up a foreign language as effortlessly as they pick up their own, if we provide them with the right opportunities.

This interactive story introduces simple French words and phrases that children can use to communicate. The story has two elements:

* the narration, which includes some French phrases for the child to recognise and understand;
* Léo the cat's simple words and phrases, that the child will soon want to repeat.

Léo's speech is on lift-up flaps, with the English translation under the flap. By lifting the flaps, the child becomes physically involved in the story. This makes learning easier, as it helps the child to confirm the meaning of each word or phrase and absorb it.

As in the initial stages of learning English, children need time to absorb French before they are ready to use it. Read the story in the same way as you read stories in English, encouraging them to join in. When they are ready they will do so, and may even surprise you by taking over Léo's role!

When you are reading the book, use a quieter voice for the English translation to indicate that it is not a vital part of the story. As the story becomes better known, the translation can be left out altogether – the child no longer needs it.

Success motivates; it also makes children happy. Be generous with praise, as what you share successfully today will influence children's attitudes to foreign language learning in the future.

Have fun together!

Opal Dunn

Look! There's Léo. Let's talk to him.
But he only speaks French, so we'll talk to him in French.
Listen.

Bonjour. *Hello.*

Let's ask him to come.

Viens. *Come.*

Viens ici. *Come here.*

He wants to play so we'll ask him to sit down.

Assieds-toi. *Sit down.*

Tu vas où? *Where are you going?*

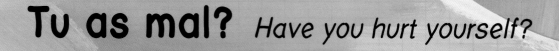

Tu as mal? *Have you hurt yourself?*

t the dog just wouldn't go away. "I
s I'll have to outrun you," said Annie.
she raced down the block. The dog looked
e didn't even try to catch up to her.

The old dog lay his head in Annie's
lap. "I'll sing you a little song," she said. The
dog liked it so much that he cheered up. He
even wagged his tail.

"Good boy." Annie smiled and patted him. "Now, I've got to find my real family. So, good-bye!" Annie walked away, but the old dog trotted along behind her.

"Listen," Annie told him. a home. I don't even have of

Bu
gues
And
sad.

Just then a dogcatcher drove up
and saw the dog. "Come here, you
old stray," he called

Then he clamped a collar around the
dog's neck. When Annie saw the dogcatcher,
she came running over.

"HEY!" she yelled. "You can't take that dog away."

"I sure can," said the dogcatcher. "He's just a stray."

"Sure, sure," laughed the dogcatcher. And he pulled the dog toward his truck.

"Aw, please, mister," Annie begged. "He's my dog. He really is."

"What's his name?" asked the dogcatcher.

"Uh—Sandy!"
Annie said quickly.

"Well," said the dogcatcher, "you run over there and call Sandy. If he comes, I'll know he's really your dog."

"Golly!" gulped Annie as she ran down the block. "I sure hope this works." She turned around and called, "Sandy! Oh, Sandy!"

But the dog didn't move. He didn't
even raise his head.

"Jeepers," sighed Annie. She decided to try
again.

"SANDY!" she shouted, as loud as she
could, "COME HERE, SANDY!"

Suddenly the dog leaped straight up! He raced right over to Annie. "Arf!" he barked.

Then he licked her face again and again.
"Good going, Sandy!" she said.

"I guess you win, little girl," said the
dogcatcher. "That dog is yours."
"Of course he is," Annie said, laughing.

She gave Sandy a great big hug.
"From now on, you and I are family. We will stay together <u>forever</u>!"

So Annie, the little girl with the red hair, and Sandy, her scruffy dog, walked away together. "Now, let's find a nice home," Annie told him. And they did!